![Daniel Tiger's Neighborhood logo]

Daniel has an Allergy

Adapted by Angela C. Santomero

Based on the screenplay "Daniel's Allergy" written by Angela C. Santomero

Poses and layouts by Jason Fruchter

Simon Spotlight

New York   London   Toronto   Sydney   New Delhi

SIMON SPOTLIGHT
An imprint of Simon & Schuster Children's Publishing Division
1230 Avenue of the Americas, New York, New York 10020
This Simon Spotlight paperback edition December 2017
© 2017 The Fred Rogers Company
SIMON SPOTLIGHT and colophon are registered trademarks of Simon & Schuster, Inc.
For information about special discounts for bulk purchases, please contact Simon & Schuster
Special Sales at 1-866-506-1949 or business@simonandschuster.com.
Manufactured in the United States of America 1117 LAK
10 9 8 7 6 5 4 3 2 1
ISBN 978-1-5344-0905-7 (pbk)
ISBN 978-1-5344-0906-4 (eBook)

It was a beautiful day in the neighborhood, and Daniel was going to make a peach pie for his class at school.

Daniel had never eaten a peach before.
"Do you want to try a peach?" asked Dad.
"Sure," said Daniel.
Daniel took a bite. It was deeeeee-licious!

Mom noticed that Daniel had some red bumps on his face. "Does anything else bother you?" asked Mom.
"My tummy kind of hurts," said Daniel.

Dad and Daniel boarded Trolley to go to Dr. Anna's office.
"Am I going to be okay?" Daniel asked.
"You're going to be okay because Dr. Anna will take care of you,"
said Dad. "She will figure out why you are itchy and why your
tummy hurts."

Daniel felt a little better. Then Dad sang, *"We take care of each other."*

Daniel and Dad arrived at Dr. Anna's office.

"What did you eat today?" Dr. Anna asked Daniel.

"I had blueberries and oatmeal for breakfast, and then I tried peaches for the first time," said Daniel.

"Ah!" said Dr. Anna. "You could be allergic to the peaches."

"Allergic?" Daniel asked.

"That means your body doesn't like peaches," Dr. Anna explained. "They give you these itchy bumps—or hives—on your face and legs, and a tummy ache when you eat them."

Dr. Anna gave Daniel some medicine that would make him feel better.

"We take care of each other," Dr. Anna sang. She was happy to help.

"But I also need you to take care of yourself," Dr. Anna said. She gave Daniel three rules to follow.

Rule 1: Don't eat the food that you're allergic to.

Rule 2: If you don't feel well, tell a grown-up.

Rule 3: Ask before you eat something new to make sure you are not allergic.

Dad and Daniel left Dr. Anna's office. Daniel felt better.

"So if someone gives me peaches, I just say 'no thank you'?" Daniel asked.

"Right," said Dad. "You can say 'yes thank you' to bananas, blueberries, and strawberries."

Daniel liked all those foods!

That gave him an idea.

Do you want to make believe with Daniel?

Daniel imagined he was in a video game. He sang a song!

Allergies! Allergies!
Pineapple, pizza,
watermelon pieces,
Daniel Tiger needs to
avoid the peaches.
Tomatoes, beets?
My favorite treats!
Bananas and toast?
I can eat both!

Allergies! Allergies!
Veggie stew? Don't
mind if I do! How about
a slice of peach? No,
that's not for me. He
doesn't eat them so
he won't feel sick.
Allergies! Allergies!

At home Daniel shared everything he learned with Mom.

But then he remembered. He was supposed to make a peach pie to bring to school!

"Oh no," Daniel sighed. "Now we can't make peach pie."

"Let's figure out something new we can bake together," said Mom.

Daniel looked around the kitchen. He saw the peaches, but he couldn't have them.

"Do you see a fruit you can have?" asked Mom.

There were lots of fruits Daniel could have. He could have oranges and apples and bananas!

"How about we make banana bread muffins?" Daniel asked.

"Good idea," said Mom. "Let's bake!"

But Daniel had never tried jam before. Thanks to his new rules, he knew what to do. He had to ask before trying something new.

"Are there peaches in this?" Daniel asked.
"This jam has no peaches," Mom told him.
Daniel put some jam on his banana muffin. It was deeeeee-licious!

I'm allergic to peaches. But my mom and dad and Dr. Anna took care of me, because we take care of each other. Are you allergic to any foods?
Ugga Mugga!

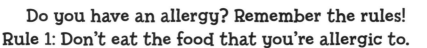

Do you have an allergy? Remember the rules!

✓ Rule 1: Don't eat the food that you're allergic to.

✓ Rule 2: If you don't feel well, tell a grown-up.

✓ Rule 3: Ask before you eat something new to make sure you are not allergic.